Printed by Great Northern Press

Published in the United States
by
Diotima Press
P.O. Box 608
Stroudsburg, PA 18360
717-476-9439

ISBN 0-9642128-0-3                    $17.95

# AMY ANGEL GOES HOME

## A Heavenly Tale of Adoption

*This book is dedicated to my husband, Dominick, and my children, Trieste, Dominick and Amelia.*

Special thanks to Shawn Queenan, Joyce Eisenberg and Trisha Rubin.

"GOO-BEE-DA-BE-DOOO!" said the Great Guardian Angel, smiling at her class in the waiting-to-be-born heaven. The little angels and cherubs laughed. "We have to do THAT!?" exclaimed little Amy Angel.

"Yes," responded the Great Guardian. "All babies talk baby-talk. You must learn the baby ways and win your three stars. Then you can be born."

O.K. with me, thought Amy. I just want to go to my new home.

"GAA-BEE-DOO-BEE-DA!" Amy said with a little giggle. A star in the sky came swirling toward her.

TWIZZLE – TWINK!

The shooting star sparkled as it landed on Amy's halo. "My first star!" shouted Amy proudly. "Two more and I can be a real BABY!"

"O-BLA-DEE-BEE-DOO?" said Charlie.

TWIZZLE – TWINK!

A bright star landed on his halo.

TWIZZLE – TWINK!

TWIZZLE – TWINK!

Shooting stars came spinning through the sky as each little angel
DOO-BEE-DOO'd and DAA-BEE-DAA'd.

The Great Guardian Angel was pleased. "Now that you all have earned your first star," she said, "you are ready to see who your parents will be. Amy, you were first, so I'll start with you. Look over here." She waved toward the clouds below and said:

*"Show me Mommy.*
*Show me Dad.*
*Amy's parents*
*will soon be glad."*

Instantly the clouds began to move and separate.

Amy saw two people. "These are the parents that God wants YOU to have, Amy," the Great Guardian Angel said.

Amy smiled and waved. "What's that?" she asked, pointing to a light shining from their hearts.

"That is the Light of Love," answered the Great Guardian. "It is a special love that parents have for their children. Your parents are waiting to share this love with you." Amy's heart tingled with love as she gazed at her future parents. "I love them, too," she whispered to herself.

The Great Guardian Angel turned to Charlie. She spread her arms towards the glowing clouds below and said:

*"Show me Mommy.*
*Show me Dad.*
*Charlie's parents*
*will soon be glad."*

They could see two more people through the clouds. "These are the parents that God wants YOU to have, Charlie," the Great Guardian Angel said softly.

"Oh, thank you!" Charlie Cherub said with delight. He saw the bright white Light of Love in their hearts. He felt his love for them begin to grow.

Then he saw the soft, round Glow of life in his mommy. He knew this Glow was the baby part of himself, growing and waiting to be born.

Meanwhile, Amy peered at her mommy and daddy. What a beautiful Light of Love, she thought, feeling the love growing in her heart. But then she noticed that her mommy did not have the Glow.

She turned to Charlie. "How can I be a baby if my mommy does not have the Glow?" she asked.

"I don't know," he answered, "but you don't have all your stars yet anyway. So don't worry. Your parents will be ready when you are."

Amy laughed. "I guess they'll have to be."

Just then, the Great Guardian Angel called the class together. "It is time to learn the hic - cups," she said. "This is tricky. Watch." The Great Guardian Angel bopped a little baby bounce. "Hic - CUP."

"Hic - Hic," Amy wiggled.

"Hic - Lic,"                    Amy jiggled.

"Hic - Luc," Amy hopped.

"Hic - CUP!" Amy bopped a perfect baby bounce.

# TWIZZLE – TWINK!

Amy's star flew to her halo. She looked around.

TWIZZLE – TWINK!    TWIZZLE – TWINK!

TWIZZLE – TWINK!

A blizzard of stars fell as each little baby-to-be bopped a perfect baby bounce with a "Hic - CUP." Now all the little angels had two stars!

"You must be tired from all the wiggles and jiggles and hopping and bopping," the Great Guardian Angel said. "It's time for a practice nap."

The angels flew to their favorite clouds. Charlie settled on a huge Tyrannosaurus Rex. Amy sat on the back of a giant eagle. Watching their parents was much more fun than sleeping.

"My mommy and daddy are getting ready for me right now," Charlie said. "Look at my new bed and the big teddy bear!"

Amy peeked through the clouds. "My parents are getting ready for me, too," she said. "See how they're holding my blanket? I just know they're thinking about me!" She could feel their love drawing her closer and closer to them.

The Great Guardian called the class together. "This final lesson is the most important one," she said. "As a newborn baby, you won't be able to talk. But your parents will know how much you love them when you do the Silent Squeeze. Now, think loving thoughts, hold your partner's finger, and SQUEEZE!"

Amy held Charlie's finger and squeezed. TWIZZLE - TWINK!
Down flew her star.

Charlie held Amy's finger and squeezed. TWIZZLE - TWINK!
Down flew his star.

TWIZZLE - TWINK!
TWIZZLE - TWINK!
TWIZZLE - TWINK!

In a lightning flash, all the angels had their third star.
"Congratulations!" the Great Guardian said to all the happy students. "Now you are ready to be born!" The class cheered as they flew to watch their parents from heaven one last time.

Amy Angel looked at her mommy and daddy again. Her heart beamed with love for them. "Still no Glow in my mommy!" she exclaimed to Charlie. "I'm ready to be a baby now, but how can I?" She began to sob. Big tears ran down her face and fell into the rain clouds below. The Great Guardian Angel heard her crying and came to help.

"Great Guardian," Amy Angel sighed. "I have all my stars and I am ready to be born, but my parents don't look like they are ready for me. When will I ever be a baby?"

"Yes, but right now it is time for Charlie to go!" the Great Guardian Angel exclaimed.

She brought them through a long tunnel of clouds to the sky-train station. Charlie boarded a big blue train with shining diamond wheels. He waved good-bye to his friends. Bright sparks flew from the sky-train as it carried Charlie home.

Amy Angel looked up at the Great Guardian. "Do I go on the train now, too?" she asked.

"Amy, you are to be adopted," responded the Great Guardian Angel. "You will go to your parents a different way. You are going by boat."

"A boat or a train... I don't care *how* I get there. I just want to go HOME," Amy replied.

She turned and saw on the horizon the huge white sails of a beautiful boat, with hundreds of angels dancing around it.

"Are they having a party?" she asked.

"Yes, Amy. This is YOUR special birthday party. Your parents have prayed and waited a long, long time for you. When you arrive, their joy will be so great that their hearts will not be able to contain their bursting Light of Love! Sparks of love will fly everywhere. These angels want to feel the special joy of your parents' love, too."

"I'm ready!" cried Amy with delight.

She got into the sailboat. The gentle rocking of the boat soon turned her thoughts into happy dreams as she fell asleep.

When Amy awoke, she was in her mommy's arms. She felt the love pouring from her parents' hearts. It covered her with warm, beautiful feelings. She saw sparks of love fly up into the heavens. Joyful angels played in their light.

I want my parents to know I love them, too, Amy thought.
Remembering the Great Guardian Angel's last lesson, she squeezed her
daddy's finger . . . and he smiled.

Years later, Amy thought she remembered . . .